THE USBORNE BOOK OF WEATHER FACTS

P9-DMJ-891

Anita Ganeri

Consultant: Roger Hunt, London Weather Centre

CONTENTS

Illustrated by Tony Gibson

Additional illustrations by
Martin Newton and Ian Jackson

Designed by Teresa Foster
Additional designs by Tony Gibson

Additional research by Chris Rice

What is weather?

Weather everywhere

The four main ingredients which cause weather are the Sun, the atmosphere, water vapour and the wind. These all work together, spreading the Sun's heat around the world and making clouds, rain and snow. Weather is an endless cycle of events. It happens all around us all the time fitting together like a jigsaw.

Where it happens

The atmosphere is like a giant blanket of air around the Earth. It is divided into layers. Weather happens in the troposphere, the layer directly above the ground. Above the Equator the troposphere is about 16 km (10 miles) deep. Mount Everest, the highest point on Earth, reaches about half way up the troposphere.

DID YOU KNOW?

Without the weather to spread the Sun's heat around the world the Tropics would get hotter and hotter and the Poles colder and colder. Nothing would be able to live on the Earth.

Heavy air

The air presses down all over the Earth. This is called air or atmospheric pressure. The weight of air pressing down on each 1 sq m (10 sq ft) of the Earth's surface is greater than that of a large elephant. Air also

presses down on our bodies but we do not feel it because breathing balances out the effect. Air pressure is greatest at ground level and gets less the higher up you go. Aircraft are specially pressurized so people can breathe.

Barometers

Barometers measure air pressure. On an aneroid barometer a needle on a dial moves as the air pressure changes. Pressure is measured in millibars (mb). At sea level pressure is usually between 900-1050 mb. Pressure can also be measured in mm (in) of mercury with a mercury barometer.

Air masses

Air masses are huge masses of air which are warm, cold, dry or moist depending on the nature of the land or sea they pass over. They cover vast areas, often some 1,000,000 sq km (386,000 sq miles), about the same size as Egypt. Air masses move over the Earth's surface and help spread the Sun's heat around the world.

Air masses

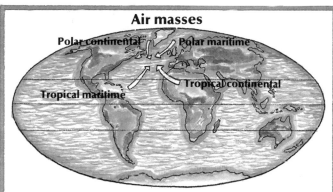

Air masses are named after the type of climate they come from. There are four main kinds:

Polar continental (cP)
Forms over very cold land like North Canada. Cold and dry in winter, warm in summer.

Polar maritime (mP)
Forms over cold Northern seas like the Arctic Ocean. Cool and showery.

Tropical continental (cT)
Comes from warm inland places like the Sahara Desert. Is hot and dry.

Tropical maritime (mT)
Forms over warm oceans near the Equator. It is warm, moist and brings unsettled weather.

Fronts

Boundaries between air masses are called fronts. Near fronts the weather can be very unsettled, with rain and clouds. Some cold fronts cause lines of violent storms, as long as 800 km (500 miles). The three types of front are warm, cold and occluded. An occluded front is where a cold front overtakes a warm one.

Highs and lows

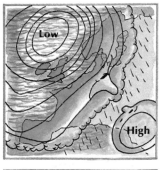

Pressure is different all over the world. Lows are areas of low pressure with the lowest pressure at the centre. Highs are areas of high pressure with the highest pressure at the centre. The way these move from day to day causes the changes in the weather. Lows usually bring wet, cloudy weather. Highs bring sunnier, dry weather.

Finding the lows

If you stand with your back to the wind in the northern hemisphere the nearest low will be on your left. In the southern hemisphere it is on your right.

3

The Sun

Energetic Sun

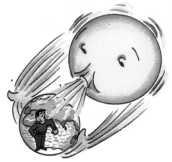

Highest recorded temperatures		
Africa	58°C	Azizia, Libya
America	57°C	Death Valley, California
Asia	54°C	Tirat Tsvi, Israel
Australia	53°C	Cloncurry, Queensland
Europe	50°C	Seville, Spain
Antarctica	14°C	Esperanza, Palmer

All the Earth's heat and light comes from the Sun. More heat and light reaches the Earth from the Sun in one minute than the whole world can produce in a year. Sunlight travels at about 300,000 km (186,000 miles) per second. It takes about 8½ minutes to reach the Earth.

Life support

The Sun keeps the temperature of most of the Earth's surface at −51°C to 49°C (−60°F to 120°F). Most living things can only survive at 0°C to 49°C (32°F to 120°F). If the amount of sunlight reaching the Earth was cut by a tenth, the oceans would turn to ice and life on Earth would die.

Effect on the weather

The Sun is the key to the world's weather. Its rays filter through the atmosphere and warm the Earth's surface which, in turn, heats the air above. The Equator is hot because the Sun shines directly overhead. The Poles are cold because the rays hit the Earth at wider angles.

DID YOU KNOW?

The light given off by a piece of the Sun's surface the size of a postage stamp is more than 500 60-watt light bulbs. It could light all the rooms in 48 average-sized homes.

The snug Earth

The Earth absorbs sunlight and then releases it into the air again as heat. The heat is trapped by water vapour and clouds in the atmosphere and reflected back to Earth. The atmosphere acts like an enormous blanket around the Earth, keeping in the warmth.

Cold mountains

People used to think that the closer you went to the Sun, the hotter it would be. But as hot air rises it expands and cools, so the higher you go the colder it is. Air cools by 3°C (5.5°F) for every 305 m (1,000 ft) it rises. This is why the tops of mountains are cold.

Lowest recorded temperatures

Antarctica	−88°C	Vostok
Asia	−68°C	Oimekon, USSR
America	−63°C	Snag, Yukon
Europe	−55°C	Ust'Schchugor, USSR
Africa	−24°C	Ilfrane, Morocco
Australia	−22°C	Charlotte Pass, NSW

Solar power

Solar panels are used to collect the Sun's heat. Water in them absorbs the heat and is used to warm homes. Electricity can also be made from sunlight. In 1982 the car *The Quiet Achiever* was driven right across Australia on sunshine power alone.

Hottest and coldest

At Dallol, Ethiopia the mean (average) shade temperature over a year is 34.4°C (94°F), making it the hottest place in the world. The coldest place in the world is Vostok in Antarctica where the mean temperature over a year is a freezing −57.8°C (−72°F).

Sunspots

Sunspots are dark patches on the Sun's surface. A single spot may be 8 times the Earth's diameter. They become very active every 11 years. Meteorologists think that sunspot activity may alter weather patterns by affecting the Earth's magnetic fields.

Thermometers

Thermometers are used to measure temperature. They are placed in the shade, 1.5 m (5 ft) off the ground. In direct sunshine and on the ground, the temperature recorded may be much higher than that off the ground.

Amazing But True

Solar ponds are lakes of salty water which collect the Sun's heat in their deepest, saltiest layers. The temperature can reach boiling point.

Scientists in New Mexico, USA proved this by boiling eggs in a solar pond. The eggs only took about five minutes to cook.

Water on the move

The world's water

About 70% of the Earth is covered with water. Most of this lies in the oceans. The Pacific Ocean alone covers almost half the world. Much of the rest of the water is in the ice sheets, glaciers and underground.

The water cycle

No new water is ever made. The rain you see has fallen millions of times before. In the water cycle the water on the Earth is used again and again. The Sun heats the oceans and lakes and millions of gallons of water rise into the air as invisible water vapour.

This is called evaporation. As the vapour rises, it cools and turns back into liquid water. This is called condensation. It falls as rain and snow and is carried back to the ocean by rivers and streams. Then the cycle begins all over again.

Water's disguises

There are 3 forms of water in the air:
1 The gas water vapour.
2 Liquid water droplets.
3 Solid ice crystals.

It changes from one form to another by evaporation, freezing, melting and condensation.

Watery air

The amount of water vapour in the air is called humidity. All air contains some water vapour but the amount varies greatly. Warm air can hold more vapour than cold air. In the Tropics the air is hot and sticky and contains nearly as much water vapour as the air in a sauna. It can be very uncomfortable.

DID YOU KNOW?

If all the water in the air fell at the same time, it would cover the whole Earth with 25 mm (1 in) of rain. This amount of rain would fill enough buckets to reach from the Earth to the Sun 57 million times.

Dew point

As air cools at night there is a point when it cannot hold any more water vapour and condensation begins. This is called the dew point and dew forms on the ground. It evaporates in the morning when the air warms up.

Dew traps

Farmers in Lanzarotte, Canary Islands, collect dew to water their crops. The dew traps look like moon craters, 3 m (10 ft) wide and 2 m (6 ft) deep. A layer of volcanic ash inside makes a good surface for condensation. Vines planted in the craters can live on the dew if it does not rain.

Rivers in the sea

Gulf Stream

West Wind Drift

→ warm
→ cold

Oceans have a great effect on climate. They absorb the Sun's heat and spread it around the world in currents. These are huge rivers in the sea driven by the winds. Warm and cold currents heat or cool the air above them causing hotter or cooler types of weather.

The oceans

The oceans supply most of the water for the water cycle. In a year up to 2,000 mm (79 in) of water evaporates from the Pacific and the Indian Oceans. It would take over a million years for the oceans' total water supply to pass through the air.

Amazing But True

The West Wind Drift carries over 2,000 times more water than the Amazon, the world's largest river. It flows three times as fast as the Gulf Stream and about 2½ times faster than the fastest man can swim.

The Gulf Stream

The warm Gulf Stream, one of the strongest currents, speeds east across the Atlantic at 178 km (111 miles) a day. It then turns north and divides, bringing mild weather to Europe. New York is only 160 km (100 miles) north of Lisbon in Portugal but in January it is cold at −1°C (31°F) while Lisbon is sunny at 10°C (50°F).

7

Clouds

How clouds form

Clouds form when warm air rises and cools down enough for some of the water vapour in it to condense into tiny water droplets or ice crystals. Billions of these make up a cloud. Water vapour can also condense on to smoke or dust specks in the air.

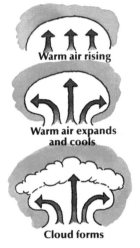

Warm air rising

Warm air expands and cools

Cloud forms

Two basic shapes

There are two basic cloud shapes caused by the two ways in which air can rise. 'Heap' (cumuliform) clouds form when bubbles of warm air rise quickly and then cool. 'Layer' (stratiform) clouds form when a large, spreading mass of air rises very slowly.

Water music

People in Chile's dry Atacama Desert collect water from sea fog. They use fog harps which are wooden frames strung with nylon threads. Water from the fog condenses on to the threads. More than 18 litres (32 pints) of water can be collected on 1 sq m (3 sq ft) of thread in a day.

Fog

Fog is really low cloud which forms when air near the ground cools. Sea fog forms when warm air from the land flows over cold seas. In the Arctic fog can rise up from the sea like steam rising from hot water. It is called sea smoke.

Fog danger

Fog reduces visibility and causes accidents on land and at sea. In 1962 two trains crashed in thick fog in London. 90 people were killed and many more injured.

8

Cloud messengers

There are three families of clouds. They were given Latin names by Luke Howard in 1804. They are cirrus ('curl of hair'), cumulus ('heap') and stratus ('layer'). There are 10 main types of clouds made up of combinations of these families. Clouds are also grouped by their height above the ground. Each cloud carries a message about the weather to come so weather men use clouds to help them make forecasts.

Cirrus

High, ice-crystal clouds which look like wispy curls of hair. Often signs of bad weather to come.

Cirrostratus

Sheets of thin, milk-coloured cloud which form high up and often bring rain within 24 hours.

Altostratus

Layers of thin, grey cloud which can grow into rain clouds. Often form haloes round the Sun.

Stratocumulus

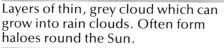

Uneven rolls or patches of cloud across the sky. Usually a sign that drier weather is on the way.

Cumulus

Clearly defined puffs of fluffy cloud like cauliflowers. They appear in sunny, summer skies.

Cirrocumulus

Often called a 'mackerel sky' – the ripples of cloud look like fish scales. Unsettled weather.

Altocumulus

Fluffy waves of grey cloud which can bring showers or break up to give sunny periods.

Nimbostratus

Thick, dark grey masses of cloud which bring rain or snow. 'Nimbus' means rain in Latin.

Stratus

Low, grey blanket of cloud which often brings drizzle. It can cover high ground and cause hill fog.

Cumulonimbus

Towering clouds which usually bring thunderstorms with rain, snow or hail.

Rainfall

Out of the clouds

Raindrops form in clouds when tiny water droplets join together or larger ice crystals melt. A raindrop must contain as many as 1,000 droplets for it to be heavy enough to fall. When water falls as rain or snow it is called precipitation.

Greatest average annual rainfalls		
Continent	MM	Place
Oceania (Pacific islands)	11,684	Mt Wai-'ale-'ale, Hawaii
Asia	11,430	Cherrapunji, India
Africa	10,277	Debundseha, Cameroon
S. America	8,991	Quibdo, Colombia
N. America	6,655	Henderson Lake, British Colombia
Europe	4,648	Grkvice, Yugoslavia
Australia	4,496	Tully, Queensland

DID YOU KNOW?

The amount of water that falls to Earth each year as rain, snow and hail is equivalent to 10 million gallons for every person in the USA. This is enough for each person to have 900 baths a day.

Raindrops and drizzle

Raindrops are usually about 1.5 mm (0.06 in) round. They never grow bigger than 5 mm (0.2 in) which is about the size of a pea. Drops less than 0.5 mm (0.02 in) round are called drizzle. Raindrops are not tear-shaped, as is often thought, but look like flat-bottomed circles.

From dry to worse

From 1570-1971 Calama, Chile held the record for being the driest place in the world. It had had no rain at all for 400 years. But on 10 February 1972 torrential rain fell causing terrible floods. The whole town was surrounded by water and its electricity supply was cut off. Many buildings were badly damaged.

Least average annual rainfalls		
Continent	MM	Place
S. America	0.8	Arica, Chile
Africa	2.5	Wadi Halfa, Sudan
N. America	30.5	Bataques, Mexico
Asia	45.7	Aden, South Yemen
Australia	119.3	Millers Creek
Europe	162.5	Astrakhan, USSR
Oceania	226.0	Puako, Hawaii

Greatest observed rainfalls		
Time	MM	Place
1 min	31	Unionville, USA
15 min	198	Plumb Point, Jamaica
12 hours	1,340	Belouve, Reunion
24 hours	1,869	Cilaos, Reunion
1 month	9,299	Cherrapunji, India
1 year	26,459	Cherrapunji, India

Most rainy days

Amazing But True

On 9 February 1859 a shower of fish fell in Glamorgan, Wales. They covered an area about the size of three tennis courts laid end to end. No one knew where they came from.

Smell of rain

Many people claim to be able to smell rain. This may be because our sense of smell is keener when the air is moist and also because of the gases given off by wet soil and plants.

Rain forests

In the tropical rain forests of South America it rains nearly every day. Each year at least 2,030 mm (80 in) and as much as 3,810 mm (150 in) of rain can fall. The air is always moist and sticky.

Rain gauge

Rain gauges measure the depth of rain which would cover the ground if none of it drained away or evaporated. The simplest type is a funnel connected to a tank which collects and measures the day's rainfall.

Rain does not fall evenly over the Earth. Mount Wai-'ale-'ale in Hawaii is the wettest place in the world. It has rain for about 335 days of the year. The annual rainfall is 11,684 mm (460 in) which would cover six people standing on each other's shoulders.

Dust Bowl

Drought is caused by a lack of rain. The Dust Bowl in America was created by years of drought from 1930-1940. The soil was so dry it was blown away by the wind and farmers were ruined. The Dust Bowl reached from Texas right to the Canadian border.

Ice and snow

What is snow?

Snow crystals form when water freezes on to ice pellets in a cloud, making them bigger. As they fall through the cloud they collide with other snow crystals and become snowflakes. Snow often melts as it passes through warmer air and falls as rain.

World snowfall records

City	Date			Amount
London	19 January	1881		4.5 m snow drifts
New York	6 February	1978		65 cm snow
Sydney	28 June	1836		Only snow on record
Jordan	2 March	1980		38 cm in Amman
Ireland	1 April	1917		25 m drifts

Snowball fight

Snow is more likely the higher you go. Some mountains are always covered in snow. In November 1958 rain fell in the New York streets while security guards on top of the Empire State Building enjoyed a snowball fight.

Snow wonder

Most snow crystals have six sides. Billions and billions have fallen to Earth but no two have ever been seen to be identical. The shape of the crystals depends on the air temperature. In colder air, needle and rod shapes form. Complicated shapes form in warmer air.

Greatest snowfall

The most snow to fall in a year was at Paradise, Mount Rainier, USA from 1971-1972. Some 31,102 mm (1,224 in) of snow fell, enough to reach a third of the way up the Statue of Liberty in New York.

Palace of ice

In 1740 the Empress of Russia built a palace of ice as a home for a newly-married prince who had disobeyed her. Everything in it was carved from ice, even the pillows on the bed. Luckily for the prince his chilly home melted in the spring.

DID YOU KNOW?

Metal pipes often burst when the water inside them turns to ice. This is because water expands when it freezes. It also becomes lighter. If ice did not float on water the seas would gradually turn to ice and no life would be able to survive on Earth.

What is hail?

Hail only falls from cumulonimbus clouds. Ice crystals are tossed up and down in the cloud as many as 25 times. Water freezes on to the crystals in layers, like the skins of an onion, until they are heavy enough to fall as hailstones. They are usually about the size and shape of peas but many unusual stones have fallen.

Lucky escape

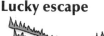

The sea between Denmark and Sweden can freeze over and the ice can be strong enough for cars to cross it. In 1716 the King of Sweden led his army over the ice to invade Denmark. The lucky Danes were saved by the ice melting.

Hail damage

Hail can badly damage crops and houses. Hailstones as big as cricket balls fell in Dallas, USA in May 1926 causing $2 million of damage in just 15 minutes. Farmers in Italy often shoot firework rockets into clouds to try to shatter the hailstones.

In 1930 five German pilots bailed out of their aircraft into a thundercloud over the Rhön mountains in Germany. They became the centres of hailstones and were bounced up and down in the cloud. Covered by layers of ice, they eventually fell frozen to the ground. Only one of the pilots survived.

Jack Frost

At night the ground cools and, in turn, cools the air around it. If the temperature falls below freezing point dew freezes and is called frost. Hoar frost often forms around keyholes and delicate fern frost on windows.

The biggest hailstone

A hailstone the size of a melon fell in Coffeyville, Kansas, USA on 3 September 1970. It weighed 750 g (1.67 lb) and was 44.5 cm (17.5 in) round.

13

Thunder and lightning

Thunderstorms

Thunderstorms usually happen when the air is warm and humid. Huge cumulonimbus clouds form in the sky and gusty winds begin to blow. A thunderstorm often lasts for less than an hour but it produces the most dramatic type of weather.

Storm survival

Lightning always takes the quickest path to the ground. Tall trees and buildings are most at risk. Very few people are struck by lightning but it is dangerous to stand near a tree in a storm. It is safest to be in a car as the lightning will go into the ground through the rubber tyres.

DID YOU KNOW?

There are about 16 million thunderstorms a year throughout the world. About 1,800 storms rage at any moment day or night.

Lightning

Electricity builds up in a thunder cloud and is released as a brilliant flash of lightning. A 'leader' stroke zig-zags to the ground. It forms a narrow path for the 'return' stroke (the one we see) to race up. Lightning can go from clouds to the ground or from cloud to cloud.

Unlucky strike

Lightning has hit the Empire State Building in New York as much as 12 times in 20 minutes and as often as 500 times a year. Most tall buildings have lightning conductors to carry the electricity safely to the ground.

Thunder

Lightning can heat the air in its path to 30,000°C (54,000°F) which is 5 times hotter than the Sun's surface. This air expands at great speed and causes the booming noise we call thunder. Thunder can be heard at least 16 km (10 miles) away.

1, 2, 3, 4, 5 . . .

Lightning and thunder happen at exactly the same time but you see lightning first because light travels faster than sound. If you hear a thunderclap 5 seconds after you see a flash, the storm is about 2 km (1.2 miles) away.

Lightning birth?

Lightning may have been one of the causes of life on Earth. Scientists in the USA sent artificial lightning through a mixture of gases similar to those in the atmosphere. Amino acids formed which are believed to be the basic ingredients found in all forms of life on Earth.

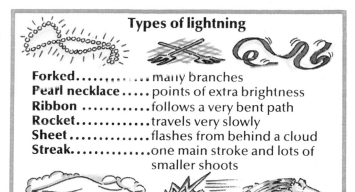

Types of lightning

Forked............many branches
Pearl necklace.....points of extra brightness
Ribbon ....follows a very bent path
Rocket............travels very slowly
Sheet.............flashes from behind a cloud
Streak.............one main stroke and lots of smaller shoots

Flash lighting

There are about 6,000 flashes of lightning every minute in the world. If the electricity from these could be collected and stored it would be enough to light every home in Britain and France for ever.

Most thundery place

Bogor in Java has at least 220 thundery days a year and has had as many as 322. It has at least 25 severe storms a year with lightning often striking a small area every 30 seconds for up to half an hour.

Ball lightning

'Fireballs' may or may not exist. There have been many reports of pear-shaped balls of fire floating into houses and then exploding. In 1980 a motorist in Britain saw a flashing ball of fire pass his car. It then exploded quite harmlessly.

Lightning speed

Lightning can travel at a speed of up to 140,000 km/s (87,000 miles/s) on its return journey. A rocket travelling at this speed would reach the Moon in 2½ seconds.

Amazing But True

The only person to survive being struck by lightning seven times was an American, Roy C. Sullivan. He lost his big toenail in 1942, his eyebrows in 1969 and had his hair set on fire twice. The other times he suffered slight burns.

World winds . . . 1

What is wind?

Wind is simply moving air. The Sun heats up some parts of the Earth more than others and the wind spreads this heat more evenly around the world. The map shows the main world and local winds.

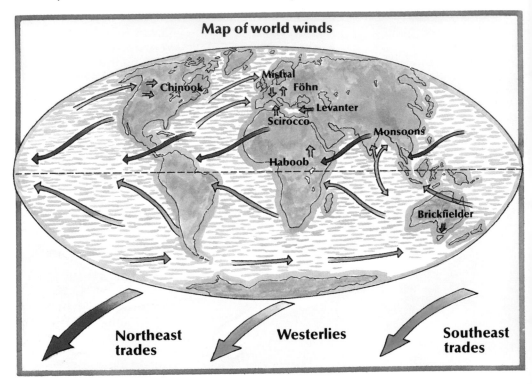

Map of world winds

Chinook · Mistral · Föhn · Levanter · Scirocco · Haboob · Monsoons · Brickfielder

Northeast trades   **Westerlies**   **Southeast trades**

How does it blow?

Air moves because of differences in pressure around the world. Warm air is light and rises leaving an area of low pressure as at the hot Equator. Cold air is heavier and sinks, causing high pressure, as at the icy Poles. Air flows from high to low pressure but it does not flow in a straight line from the Poles to the Equator. It is swung sidewards by the Earth's spin.

In a spin

The Earth spins on its axis and this affects the direction of the wind. In the northern hemisphere winds are swung to the right, and in the southern to the left. This is called the Coriolis effect.

cold air

warm air

cold air

DID YOU KNOW?

In the northern hemisphere winds flow from west to east. This means that an aircraft flying from New York to London could arrive about ½ hour early because it has the wind behind it. But it could be delayed by ½ hour on the way back when flying into the wind.

Trade winds

The trade winds are steady winds flowing towards the Equator. In the 18th century sailing ships used them as guides for crossing the Atlantic Ocean. Columbus might never have discovered America in 1492 without the trade winds' help.

Jet streams

Jet streams are very strong winds blowing about 10 km (6 miles) above the Earth. They can be up to 4,000 km (2,500 miles) long but no more than 500 km (310 miles) wide. They were not discovered until World War II when pilots found their air speed reduced when they were flying against the jet stream.

Sea breezes

On a hot, sunny day the land heats up more quickly than the sea. Because of this air rises over the land and cool sea breezes rush in to replace it.

By evening sea breezes can reach 200 km (322 miles) inland. At night land cools down more quickly than the sea so the breeze blows out from land to sea.

Amazing But True

Rising air currents called thermals can delay the fall of a parachutist. On 26 July 1959 an American pilot ejected from his plane at 14,400 m (47,000 ft) and took 40 minutes to fall through a thunder cloud instead of the expected 11 minutes.

Local winds

Winds affect the weather and are given special names in many parts of the world.

Brickfielder	Very hot NE summer wind that blows dust and sand across Australia.
Chinook	Warm, dry wind of the Rocky Mountains, USA. Welcomed by cattlemen because it can remove snow cover very quickly. Named after a local Indian tribe.
Föhn	Warm, dry European wind that flows down the side of mountains.
Haboob	The Arabic name for a violent wind which raises sandstorms, especially in North Africa.
Levanter	Pleasant, moist E wind that brings mild weather to the Mediterranean.
Mistral	Violent, dry, cold, NW wind that blows along the coasts of Spain and France.
Scirocco	Hot, dry S wind that blows across North Africa from the Sahara. Becomes very hot and sticky as it reaches the sea.

World Winds ...2

The Beaufort Scale

The Beaufort Scale was invented in 1805 by Admiral Beaufort to estimate wind speed.

The original scale was for use at sea but it has been adapted for use on land.

Force	Strength	Kph	Effect
0	Calm	0-1	Smoke rises vertically
1	Light air	1-5	Smoke drifts slowly
2	Light breeze	6-11	Wind felt on face; leaves rustle
3	Gentle breeze	12-19	Twigs move; light flag unfurls
4	Moderate breeze	20-29	Dust and paper blown about; small branches move
5	Fresh breeze	30-39	Wavelets on inland water; small trees move
6	Strong breeze	40-50	Large branches sway; umbrellas turn inside out
7	Near gale	51-61	Whole trees sway; difficult to walk against wind
8	Gale	62-74	Twigs break off trees; walking very hard
9	Strong gale	75-87	Chimney pots, roof tiles and branches blown down
10	Storm	88-101	Trees uprooted; severe damage to buildings
11	Violent storm	102-117	Widespread damage to buildings
12	Hurricane	Over 119	Devastation

The Beaufort Scale for use on land

DID YOU KNOW?

A wind that blows as fast as the fastest man can run (43 kph/27 mph), is only a 'strong breeze' on the Beaufort Scale. A wind as fast as a running cheetah (113 kph/70 mph), the world's fastest animal, registers as a 'storm'.

Blowing in the wind

Wind speed and strength must be allowed for when new buildings are designed. The bridge over the Tacoma Narrows in the USA shook so violently in strong winds that it was nicknamed 'Galloping Gertie'. It eventually collapsed during a severe storm.

Windblown

Ship designers are now going back to building sailing ships to take advantage of the wind. In August 1980, a Japanese tanker, the *Shinaltoku Maru*, was launched. As well as an engine it had two square sails, controlled by computer.

Amazing But True

Wind chill is the cooling effect of the wind on the skin. The stronger the wind the more heat is lost from the body and the colder a person feels. If human skin were exposed to winds of 48 kph (30 mph) in a temperature of −34°C (−30°F) it would freeze solid in 30 seconds.

Wind power

Windmills were once used to grind wheat to make flour. Today they are being used to generate electricity. The windmill at Tvind, Denmark is over 50 m (164 ft) high with three blades, each weighing over 5 tonnes. It can produce enough electricity to light up about 120 homes.

Windiest place

The windiest place in the world is the George V Coast in Antarctica. Here gales of 320 kph (200 mph) have been recorded.

Highest recorded gust

On 12 April 1934 a gust of wind blowing at 371 kph (231 mph) was recorded at Mount Washington, USA. This is some 251 kph (155 mph) stronger than Beaufort Scale 12, three times as strong as a hurricane.

Wind palace

The Wind Palace in Jaipur, India was specially built in the 1760s by the king so that the wind would cool it naturally. The palace is little more than a screen with balconies. The ladies of the court could sit behind these and watch the busy city down below.

Hat trick

Because wind funnels through mountains it may be stronger in a pass than on a peak. At Pali Lookout near Honolulu, a sightseer can throw his hat over the cliff and the wind will immediately throw it back.

Hurricanes

Tropical terrors

Hurricanes begin over warm, tropical oceans. They are like giant spinning wheels of storm clouds, wind and rain and can be up to 500 km (310 miles) across with winds whirling at up to 300 kph (190 mph). They sweep westwards over warm tropical seas, dying down when they reach land.

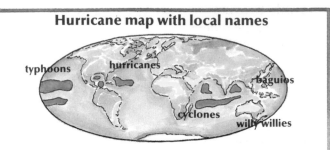

Hurricane map with local names

Hurricanes turn anti-clockwise north of the Equator and clockwise to the south.

Stormy eyes

A hurricane has a centre or 'eye'. It can be up to 32 km (20 miles) across. Here the weather is surprisingly calm with low winds and clear skies. As the 'eye' passes overhead there is a lull in the storm for a few minutes or at the most a few hours.

I name you...

Hurricanes were first given names in the 19th century by Clement Wragge, an Australian weather man. Nicknamed 'Wet Wragge', he used the names of people he had quarrelled with for very violent storms. Today an alphabetical list of names is drawn up each year for the coming year's hurricanes.

DID YOU KNOW?

If all the energy from one hurricane in a single day could be converted into electricity, it would be enough to supply the whole of the USA for three years. This is equivalent to the amount of energy needed to power 1,095 cars an incredible 36,000 times around the world.

5 of the worst recent hurricanes

Name	Date		Location	Effect
Unnamed	November	1970	Bangladesh	1 million dead
Tracey	December	1975	Darwin, Australia	90% of people homeless
David	August	1979	Dominica, W. Indies	2,000 dead; 20,000 homeless
Frederic	August	1979	Alabama, USA	£250 million damage
Allen	August	1980	Haiti	½ million homeless

Tornadoes

Terrible twisters

Tornadoes are funnel-shaped storms which twist as hot air spins upwards. At the centre winds can reach 644 kph (400 mph). Tornadoes leapfrog across land causing great damage when they touch the ground. They can suck up anything in their path, even people. Mid-West America has the most tornadoes.

Picked clean

Several chickens had all their feathers plucked off by a tornado in Bedfordshire, England in May 1950 . . . and they survived!

Tornado on tour

On 26 May 1917, a single tornado sped 471 km (293 miles) across Texas, USA. It travelled at 88-120 kph (55-75 mph) for about 7 hours and 20 minutes.

Most destructive

Tornadoes are much smaller than hurricanes but much more violent. The tornado which hit Missouri, USA in March 1925 was only 274 m (900 ft) across. It killed 800 people and uprooted trees, swept cars over rooftops and hurled aside trains.

Amazing But True

On 4 September 1981 a tornado hit Ancona in Italy. It lifted a baby asleep in its pram 15 m (50 ft) into the air and set it down safely 100 m (328 ft) away. The baby was still sleeping soundly!

Train thief

A tornado in Minnesota, USA in 1931 lifted an 83-tonne train 25 m (80 ft) into the air and dropped it in a ditch. Many of its 117 passengers died.

Highest waterspout

Waterspouts are like tornadoes but these funnels of water form over sea. The highest seen was in 1898 in Australia. It was 1,528 m (5,015 ft) high and 31 m (10 ft) across.

Climate and the seasons

What is climate?

Climate is the usual pattern of weather a place has measured over a very long time. How hot or cold a place is depends on how far north or south of the Equator it is (its latitude). Ocean currents, winds and mountains also affect climate.

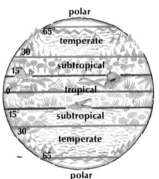

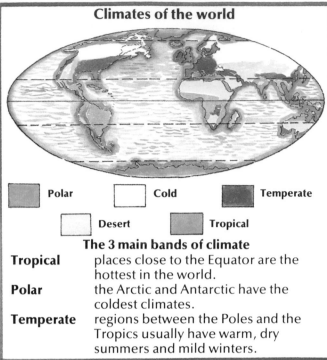

Climates of the world

Polar | Cold | Temperate

Desert | Tropical

The 3 main bands of climate

Tropical — places close to the Equator are the hottest in the world.

Polar — the Arctic and Antarctic have the coldest climates.

Temperate — regions between the Poles and the Tropics usually have warm, dry summers and mild winters.

Land and sea

Coasts have a maritime climate. Sea temperature does not change much during the year so summers are cool but winters mild. Land far from the sea heats up and cools down more quickly so summers are hotter but winters colder. This is a continental climate.

DID YOU KNOW?

Temperate climates are thought to be the most pleasant to live in as they do not usually have extremes of hot or cold. Only 7% of the Earth's land surface has a temperate climate, yet nearly half the world's population lives in these areas.

City climates

In many places with a temperate climate the west end of a city is more fashionable than the east. This is because the wind usually blows from the west bringing fresh air to the west end and carrying smoke and pollution to the eastern side.

Extreme climates

Hottest and driest

Deserts are the hottest and driest places on Earth. In some deserts rain never falls. During the day it can be hot enough to fry an egg on the sand and at night cold enough for water to freeze.

Coldest

The Antarctic is the coldest and windiest place in the world with temperatures falling well below −50°C (−60°F). Even in midsummer, temperatures stay below freezing point.

Wettest

Near the Equator much of the land is covered in dense rain forest. The temperature is about 27°C (80°F) all year round. Heavy rain falls here every day.

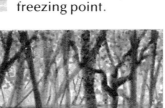

Most pleasant climate

Quito in Equador has earned the name 'Land of eternal spring' because of its climate. Temperatures never fall below 8°C (46°F) at night and reach 22°C (72°F) in the day. Every month about 100 mm (4 in) of refreshing rain falls.

Mountain sides

Mountains can affect the climate far away from them by diverting winds and rain. The sheltered (leeward) side of a mountain has dry weather because the air releases its rain as it rises up over the other (windward) side and cools.

Seasons

The seasons are caused by the Earth moving around the Sun and tilting at an angle to the Sun. They change as each half of the Earth leans towards or away from the Sun. When it is summer in the northern hemisphere it is winter in the south.

Tropical season

Summer and winter are unknown in places near the Equator as the Equator never tilts away from the Sun. Some places have dry seasons and wet or monsoon seasons, others just hot and wet.

Special effects

Rainbows

If sunlight shines through drops of water it breaks up into its 7 main colours – red, orange, yellow, green, blue, indigo and violet. When sunlight hits raindrops or water spray a rainbow appears. To see a rainbow you must have your back to the Sun. From the ground you only see part of a full circle of colours.

Long bow

Rainbows usually only last for a few minutes. But a rainbow seen in Wales on 14 August 1979 was said to have lasted for three hours.

DID YOU KNOW?

Sometimes double rainbows can form. In a single bow red is always at the top and violet at the bottom. In the second fainter bow the colours are always the other way round.

St Elmo's fire

'St Elmo's fire' is a type of lightning which clings to ships' masts and the wing tips of aircraft. It is bluish-green or white and was named after a 4th century Italian bishop, Elmo, the patron saint of fire. Sailors prayed to him for protection at sea and took 'St Elmo's fire' to be a sign of good luck whenever it appeared.

Rings round the Sun

Whitish haloes round the Sun or Moon appear when light is bent by ice crystals in clouds high up in the atmosphere. Haloes are thought to be signs that rain is on its way and this is often

true. The Zuni Indians of North America believed that when the Sun was 'in his tepee' (that is, inside a halo) rain was likely to follow shortly afterwards.

Diamond dust

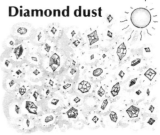

In very cold climates when temperatures drop to below −30°C (−22°F) water droplets in fog may freeze and the air fills with ice crystals. These fall slowly to the ground sparkling in the sunshine and are called ice fog or 'diamond dust'. It is dangerous if breathed in.

Mirages

Mirages are optical illusions. Light is bent as it passes through layers of air with different densities so distant objects look distorted.

Mirages are often seen over hot deserts or roads where a layer of heavy cold air lies over a layer of light warm air. Water may seem to appear on roads but this is really only the light from the sky reflected as if in a mirror. A similar reflection causes oases to appear in the desert.

Fata Morgana

One of the most beautiful mirages is the Fata Morgana, named after a fairy in a story. The mirage appears in the Strait of Messina, Italy as a town in the sky. Then a second town appears piled on top of the first, then a third. Each has splendid palaces and tall towers. People dressed in white seem to walk through the streets. No-one is sure what the mirage reflects but it may be one of the small fishing villages on the coast.

Amazing But True

Some fabulous animals were seen in the Gobi Desert by an American explorer, Roy Chapman Andrews. They looked like giant swans wading in a lake on legs 4½ m (15 ft) long. As Andrews went nearer, the water disappeared and the creatures changed shape. The giant swans were really antelopes grazing on the grass.

Red skies

At sunrise and sunset the sky is often a rich orange-red colour. This is because the short blue light waves in sunlight are scattered by dust in the air and only the longer red waves can get through. The colour of the sky is thought to show what the weather will be like. A red sky at night is said to be a sign of a fine day to come and a red sunrise a sign of bad weather.

Measuring the weather

Weather watching

There are about 10,000 weather stations all over the world in cities, at airports and on weather ships. Working together they watch the weather very closely. Every few hours they measure

humidity, wind speed and direction, pressure and temperature and check rain gauges. All this information is translated into an international code and sent round the world for forecasters to use.

Eureka

The Eureka weather station in Canada is the most remote in the world. It is 960 km (600 miles) from the North Pole – further north than any Eskimos live. Built in 1947, it has many luxuries including a greenhouse where staff grow plants during the 5 months when there is constant daylight.

Radiosonde

The weather high up in the atmosphere affects the weather on Earth. To measure it, balloons are sent up carrying instruments which radio information back to the ground. The balloons reach heights of 35-40 km (20-25 miles) and then burst. Small parachutes carry the instruments safely back to the ground.

Satellites

Satellites show weather patterns which cannot be seen from the ground. There are two types of weather satellites. Polar orbitting

satellites circle the Earth while geo-stationary satellites stay in a fixed place 35,000 km (22,000 miles) above the Equator. Cameras on board send back photographs of clouds.

Weather firsts

The first weather satellite was *Tiros I*, launched on 1 April 1960. It circled the Earth every two hours at heights of 700-1500 km (420-900 miles) and sent back pictures of cloud and snow cover.

Radar

Using radar, weathermen can see if rain is on the way. Each radar covers an area of about 200 km (124 miles) and picks up echo signals of the rain. On the radar screen the white patches are rain.

Storm tracking

In the USA radar is used to follow storms minute by minute so that tornado warnings can be given. In 1985 the Wimbledon tennis championships were saved by radar which saw a terrible storm coming. The groundstaff were warned in time to cover the courts.

Instruments for measuring weather

Weather	Instrument	Units
Atmospheric pressure	Barometer	Millibars
Temperature	Thermometer	°C/°F
Rainfall	Rain gauge	mm
Sunshine	Campbell Stokes recorder	Hours
Wind speed	Anemometer	Kph
Wind direction	Wind vane/wind sock	NSEW
Humidity	Wet bulb thermometer	°C/°F

Cloud cover

The amount of cloud covering the sky is measured in eighths (oktas) from 1 to 8 oktas. 0 oktas means the sky is clear, 8 means it is completely covered. The height of a cloud is measured by how far its base is above sea level.

Anemometer

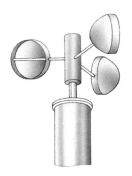

Anemometers measure wind speed. The most common type looks like a toy windmill. Three cups are fixed to a central shaft and the stronger the wind blows the faster they spin round. The wind speed in kph (mph) is shown on a dial, just like a car's speedometer.

Forecasting the weather

Sign language

People were predicting the weather long before forecasts appeared on T.V. or in newspapers. They looked for 'signs' in the way plants and animals behave. When the pressure drops – a sign of bad weather – sheeps' wool uncurls and ants move to higher ground. Pine cones open when rain is about.

Weather maps

A forecaster is like a detective gathering information and clues. Detailed information about the weather at a certain time of the day is collected and plotted on a map, called a synoptic chart. From this the forecaster, using a computer, can work out very accurately what the next day's weather should be like.

Amazing But True

Animals can indicate the weather, often very accurately. The Germans used to keep frogs as live barometers because they croak when the pressure drops.

Isobars

Isobars are lines drawn on a synoptic chart joining together areas of equal pressure. The further apart they are, the lighter the wind. When they are close together the pressure is usually low and the wind is strong.

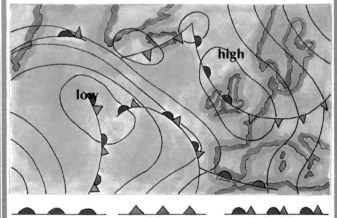

| warm front | cold front | occluded front |

Early warning

As long ago as the 5th century BC the Greeks sent out weather forecasts to their sailors. In the 4th century BC calendars of weather facts and forecasts called 'peg' calendars were put up on important buildings in many Greek cities and were very popular.

DID YOU KNOW?

The more observations there are the more accurate the forecasts will be. Ideally scientists would need frequent reports for every 15 cm² (2.3 in²) of the Earth's surface. This means a report for each piece of the Earth just big enough to stand on.

Forecast factory

An English man, L. R. Richardson, was one of the first people to try to forecast the weather using mathematical equations. He worked out though that he would need a staff of 64,000 to do all the sums quickly enough.

Record forecasts

The U.S. Weather Service makes about 2 million forecasts a year. It also sends out storm and flood warnings and nearly 750,000 forecasts for aircraft. It claims that its one day forecasts are accurate more than three quarters of the time.

Computer age

Because computers can do difficult sums very quickly they have made forecasting much more accurate. The two largest computers are at the weather centres in Washington, USA and Bracknell, UK. The Bracknell computer can handle 400 million calculations a second.

False alarm

In 1185 an astronomer, Johannes of Toledo, predicted that the following year a terrible wind would bring famine and destruction to Europe. People were so frightened that some built new homes underground. But nothing happened!

Who uses forecasts?

Forecasts are used everyday to help us decide what to wear and where to go. They are vital to pilots, sailors and farmers who need to know exactly what weather to expect. If cold weather is on the way more electricity is made and chemists stock more cold cures. Dairies make more ice-cream if hot weather is expected.

Two types of forecast

There are two types of forecast – short and long range. Computers help forecasters produce short range charts for up to a week ahead. Long range forecasting is less accurate and is often done by looking at past weather records. In India forecasts have been made of the next year's monsoon so that famine can be prevented if the rain fails as often happens.

Weather wear and tear

Wear and tear

Rain, wind and frost are always wearing away the Earth's surface. This is called weathering. Rain collects in cracks in the rocks. If it freezes it expands and cracks the rocks apart with a force of 90 kg (200 lb) per 6 sq cm (1 sq in) to form crevices. The wind carries away small pieces of rock chipped off when crevices form.

Wind on sand

Sand blown by the wind helps to shape deserts. Wind blowing constantly from one direction piles the sand up into sanddunes. As more sand is blown across the top of a dune and trickles down the other side, the dune rolls forward like a wave. Small dunes can move more than 15 m (50 ft) a year and can bury whole villages as they pass. The two main types of dune are barchan and seif. The much larger seif dunes can be up to 400 km (250 miles) long.

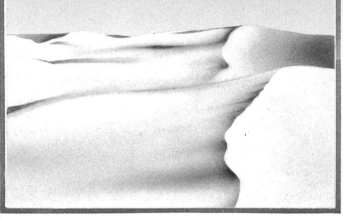

DID YOU KNOW?

Weathering is very slow. The height of some mountains is lowered by about 8.6 cm (3½ in) every 1,000 years. At this rate a mountain only as tall as the Eiffel Tower would take over 3 million years to wear right down.

Highest dunes

The highest measured sanddunes in the world are in the Sahara Desert. They can reach a height of 430 m (1410 ft) – nearly as high as the Empire State Building in New York, USA.

Sand saucers

Huge 'saucers' have been scooped out of the Sahara Desert by windblown sand. The Qattara Depression in Egypt is a huge hollow area below sea-level which is almost the size of Wales.

Fairy forest

Trees growing very high up on mountain sides have to grow close to the ground for protection from the strong cold wind. They are forced to grow sideways and become twisted. These are called krummholz trees or elfin wood. Some fir and pine trees grow so close to the ground that you can step right over them.

Irrigation

In places with little rainfall, water is stored in reservoirs and tanks and used for crops and for drinking. In the USA irrigation accounts for nearly half of the water used. The world's longest irrigation canal is in the USSR. It is 850 km (528 miles) long, over twice as long as Britain's River Thames.

Weather and crops

Temperature and rainfall are the most important influences on growing crops. There is an ideal climate for every crop and farmers have to consider their local climate before choosing which are the best crops to grow.

Weather beaters

Scientists are now at work creating crops which can survive in harsh climates. These include potatoes and sugar beet which can live through droughts and barley which is not killed by frost.

Ice slice

Glaciers are huge rivers of ice which move slowly down mountain slopes. In the last Ice Age rocks in the underside of the ice scraped and tore away deep valleys like the Norwegian fjords.

Crops and climate

Crop	Ideal climate
oranges	warm and sunny
rice	warm and wet
maize	warm and wet in summer
oats	quite cool and wet
potatoes	cool and wet

Living with the weather

Weather wear

People wear clothes suited to the climate they live in. In hot places like the Middle East they wear long, loose robes specially folded so that cool air is trapped inside. In the desert people wear turbans and veils to protect their heads and faces from the Sun and sand. Fur is worn in cold places because it is very good at keeping out the cold.

DID YOU KNOW?

The hot, dry Föhn and Scirocco winds are said to damage the health. During the Föhn the accident, crime and suicide rates in Germany rise. The Scirocco is said to cause madness.

Aches and pains

There may be some truth in the saying that people can feel the weather in their bones. Some people find that they have aches and pains when the air is humid. Others get headaches before a thunderstorm.

Body guard

The body protects itself from too much heat or cold by perspiring or shivering. Shivering is caused by the muscles twitching and giving off heat. Perspiration is the body's own air-conditioner. It evaporates off the skin and cools it down.

Lifestyles

Weather affects the way people live. In the desert people such as the Bedouins of the Sahara live a nomadic life. They move from place to place in search of water and fodder for their animals. They live in tents to make moving house easier.

Windcatchers

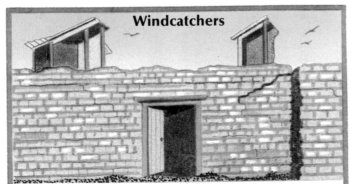

In the hot climate of Pakistan many houses have windcatchers on their roofs. These trap the wind and direct it down into the house to keep it cool. They are a simple but very effective system of natural air-conditioning.

Sleepy head

Animals react to changes in the weather. Some hibernate in winter when food is short. Their pulse and breathing rates slow down to save energy. A hibernating hedgehog only breathes once every 6 seconds – 200 times slower than its normal breathing rate.

Water frog

The water-holding frog which lives in the Central Australian Desert only has a drink every five to six years. This is how often rain falls. Then the frog comes to the surface and absorbs about half its own weight in water so it looks like a small balloon. This supply keeps the frog alive during the droughts.

The higher you go the thinner the air and the harder it is to breathe. But people have been able to adapt. Andean Indians, living in mountain villages at about 5,200 m (17,000 ft) have larger lungs and hearts than normal so they can breathe properly even at this great height.

Skin shield

People who live in hot climates have darker skins to protect them from the Sun. Their skin contains a lot of melanin, a brown pigment which acts as a shield against the Sun's harmful ultra-violet rays. Fair-skinned people tend to get sunburnt easily as they are not so well protected.

Ice house

Eskimos used to build their homes out of snow to make use of the Arctic climate they live in. Igloos are quick to build. Blocks of snow are made into a circular base then more circles are added on top, each smaller than the last. An air hole is left at the top and an entrance tunnel built. Snow is such a good insulator that it keeps the inside of the igloo warm and snug though the outside walls stay frozen.

Changing the weather

Warmly wrapped

Most scientists think that the Earth is getting warmer. Burning coal, oil and forests increases the amount of the gas carbon dioxide in the atmosphere. This acts like a giant blanket round the Earth keeping in warmth which would otherwise escape. If the amount of carbon dioxide in the air was doubled the Earth's temperature would rise by 2°C (4°F).

Some scientists think that the Earth is getting colder as more pollution in the air blocks out more of the Sun's heat. They have thought of some unusual ways to prevent a new Ice Age.

One of their ideas is to spread vast black plastic sheets or layers of soot over the Polar ice caps. The black surface would absorb heat from the Sun and cause the ice to melt.

If the ice melted

If the Earth became even a few degrees warmer the ice at the Poles would melt and the sea-level rise by about 60 m (200 ft). Coastal cities like New York, Bombay, London and Sydney would be drowned.

Fog clearing

Fog can cause accidents and delays at airports. Many airports today have huge pipes along the sides of the runways. Fuel is pumped into them and burned. This raises the air temperature so that the fog evaporates and planes can take off and land safely.

Acid rain

The rain which falls on parts of Europe and North America can be more acid than lemon juice. Acid rain falls when gases and chemicals from factories dissolve in water in the air to form weak acids. Pollution carried by the wind can fall as acid rain hundreds of kilometers away and destroy forests, crops and life in lakes and rivers.

Traffic trouble

In many big cities the air is being polluted by exhaust fumes from cars, lorries and buses. Smog, a mixture of smoke and fog, forms when these fumes react with sunlight. In Los Angeles, USA and Tokyo, Japan thick smog is a serious problem. It can damage people's health and destroy stone buildings and crops.

Pea-soupers

Until the 1960s London had terrible, thick smogs called pea-soupers which were coloured green by smoke from factories and coal fires. The worst pea-souper was in December 1952. Some 4,000 people died from bronchitis and pneumonia.

Making rain

To make artificial rain, crystals of silver iodide are shot into clouds from aircraft. Water in the cloud freezes round them and falls as rain or snow. No-one knows how well this works.

Aerosol cans used for hairsprays and paints may be harmful. They contain gases called freons which, some scientists think, destroy the gas ozone 24 km (15 miles) up in the atmosphere. Without the ozone layer we would die because it protects us from the Sun's harmful ultra-violet rays.

Rain forests

Every three seconds a piece of South American rain forest the size of a football pitch is cut down. This may lead to changes in rainfall and temperature around the world. Trees 'breathe out' water vapour which is turned into rain in the water cycle. Destroying the forests means that less water vapour is made and less rain falls. Burning the trees increases the amount of carbon dioxide in the air and may be making the Earth warmer.

Weather of the past

Ice Ages

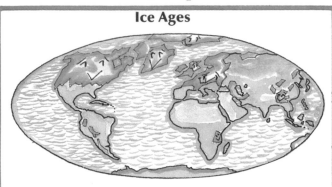

The Earth's climate changes very slowly over the centuries. It is made up of warm periods (interglacials) and cold periods (glacials) or Ice Ages. We live in an interglacial which began about 10,000 years ago. The last glacial was 19,000 years ago when a third of the Earth lay under an ice sheet some 244 m (800 ft) thick.

How Ice Ages happen

Ice Ages are caused by changes in the Earth's orbit round the Sun. Even the tiniest difference in the Earth's path can alter the amount of heat the Earth receives from the Sun and plunge it into a freezing Ice Age.

DID YOU KNOW?

A change in climate may have been the reason for dinosaurs becoming extinct about 65 million years ago. At this time, some people believe, a meteor struck the Earth causing a dust cloud to block out the Sun's heat and the Earth became very cold. Dinosaurs were probably cold-blooded and so froze to death.

Ice cores

One way of finding out about past climates is by drilling holes in glaciers and pulling out long cores of ice. Distinct layers can be seen in the ice. The darker the ice the colder the climate was. An ice core 366 m (1200 ft) long can tell us about the weather of the past 1400 years.

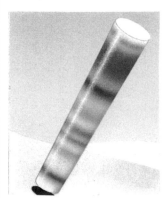

Climate clues

Scientists find clues about the Earth's past in fossils, soils and trees. Every year a tree grows a new ring. If the ring is wide the weather was

moist and warm, if narrow then it was dry and cold. Tree ring dating gives the most reliable picture of the weather of the past. Bristlecone pines in the USA give the longest record. Some are over 4,000 years old.

Viking voyages

From AD 1000-1200 the world's weather became warmer. The Arctic ice melted and the Vikings were able to sail north from Scandinavia to Greenland which was about 1-4°C (2-7°F) warmer than today. They also sailed across the Atlantic to North America. Today's storms and icebergs would make this route very dangerous for the light, wooden Viking boats.

Frost fairs

Little Ice Age

From about AD 1400 the Earth's climate became much colder and the 'Little Ice Age' began. In the winter of 1431 every river in Germany froze over. The cold weather lasted until about 1850. Arctic pack ice stretched towards the Equator and the temperature was about 2-4°C (4-7°F) lower than today.

During the Little Ice Age the River Thames in London froze over in winter and fairs were held on the ice. The first was in 1607. Tents were set up and there were swings, foodstalls and sideshows. In the winter of 1683 the ice was 26 cm (10 in) thick. The last frost fair was in 1813. It only lasted a few days but the ice was strong enough for an elephant to walk on.

Saharan seasons

About 450 million years ago the Sahara Desert was covered in ice. But from about 4000-2000 BC it was covered in grass and trees. Cave paintings from Tassili, Algeria which date from that time, show people hunting and lions, buffalo and elephants roaming wild.

Amazing But True

London, England was a very different place 50 million years ago. It had a hot, humid climate and was covered in marshy swamps and tropical jungle where hippos, turtles and crocodiles lived.

Weather gods

Weather power

Good harvests depend on good weather. Early farmers, such as the Sumerians, who lived 7,000 years ago, thought gods ruled the weather. These gods were worshipped with prayers and sacrifices. People today still pray for fine weather and for a good harvest.

Blood-thirsty Sun

The Aztecs believed that the Sun god, Huitzilopochti, was a warrior who fought against the power of night so that the Sun could be reborn every morning. He had to be kept strong and people were sacrificed to provide him with human hearts and blood which were thought to be his favourite food.

Some early primitive people thought that evil spirits lived in the clouds who sent down hail to destroy their crops. They used to shoot arrows into the clouds to frighten the spirits away.

Wind worship

The Ancient Greeks gave the winds names and characters. The Tower of the Winds in Athens, built in 100 BC, shows one of the eight main winds on each wall. Each is dressed for the weather it brings.

Boreas (North)
Notos (South)
Zephyros (West)
Apeliotes (East)
Kaikas (North East)
Euros (South East)
Lips (South West)
Skiros (North West)

Re and Nut

Like the Aztecs, the Ancient Egyptians believed that the gods ruled everything in nature. Their most important god was Re, the Sun god whose mother, Nut, was the sky goddess. Nut was held up by the god of air who stood over the god of Earth.

Sun kings

Many people have worshipped the Sun as the source of life itself. The Ancient Egyptians even believed that their Pharoah was the son of the Sun god, and in Japan the Emperor was thought to be a direct descendant of the Sun goddess.

Thunderous Thor

Thor was the Norse god of thunder. He was thought to be very strong and have wild red hair and a beard. Thor raced across the sky in a chariot pulled by two giant goats and brewed up storms by blowing through his beard. He lived in a great hall called Bilskirnir which means lightning.

Dragon breath

The Chinese believed that dragons formed clouds with their breath and brought rain. The rain fell when the dragons walked over the clouds and storms raged when they fought with each other.

Hot dog days

The Romans called the hottest days of summer 'dog days'. They linked the weather with the stars, and at this time Sirius, the Dog star, was the brightest in the sky.

Chinese calendar

In the 3rd century BC the Chinese divided the year into 24 festivals connected with the weather. Each season had six festivals telling people what weather to expect so that they could sow and harvest their crops at the right times.

Rainbow god

The Kabi people from Queensland in Australia worship a god called Dhakhan who is half fish and half snake. Dhakhan lives in deep water holes in the ground. He appears as a rainbow in the sky when he moves from one hole to the next.

Dancing in the rain

The Hopi Indians of North America perform special rain dances like the buffalo and snake dances. As they dance they pray to the gods to send them rain.

Water everywhere

There are many stories about a great flood which nearly destroyed mankind. The Bible tells of Noah and the Ark. In the Babylonian poem 'Gilgamesh' a violent storm drowns the Earth. In the Greek myth Zeus sends the flood to punish people for being so wicked.

Freaks and disasters

Iced turtle

During a severe hailstorm on 11 May 1894 near Vicksburg, USA a gophar turtle the size of a brick fell with the hail. It had been bounced up and down in a thunder cloud and coated in layer after layer of ice.

Worst weather disasters			
Disaster	Location	Date	Deaths
Drought/famine	Bengal, India	1943-4	1,500,000
Flood	Henan, China	1939	1,000,000
Hurricane	Bangladesh	1970	1,000,000
Smog	London, UK	1952	2,850
Tornado	Missouri, USA	1925	800
Hail	Moredabad, India	1888	246
Lightning	Umtali, Zimbabwe	1975	21

Amazing But True

On 14 October 1755 rain the colour of blood fell in Locarno, Switzerland and red snow fell over the Alps. This odd colouring was caused by dust from the Sahara Desert in North Africa which had been carried over 3,000 km (1,850 miles) by the wind.

Desert snow

Snow fell in the Kalahari Desert in Africa on 1 September 1981 – the first time in living memory. Temperatures dropped as low as $-5°C$ (23°F).

Leg strike

Lightning can fuse or melt metal together. On 10 August 1975 a cricket umpire in England was struck by lightning. He was not hurt but the knee joint in his false metal leg was welded quite solid!

Food from the sky

The sky over Turkey rained down food in August 1890. A type of edible lichen fell with the rain which the local people collected and made into bread.

Hot and cold

On 22 January 1943 a freezing cold winter's day in South Dakota, USA was transformed into a balmy spring one. At precisely 7.30 in the morning the temperature rose an amazing 27°C (49°F) in just two minutes.

Out of the blue

Thirty workers picking peppers in Arizona, USA were knocked down by a flash of lightning which appeared out of a clear sky. Three died and many were injured.

About turn

A tornado in the USA picked up a railway engine, turned it round in mid-air and put it down again on a parallel track running in the other direction.

Watery walkways

The captain of a ship bound for Uruguay in 1929 reported seeing the unique sight of two large clouds connected by two waterspouts. Waterspouts have often been mistaken for sea monsters.

Pennies from heaven

In June 1940 a shower of silver coins fell in Gorky, USSR. A tornado uncovered an old treasure chest, lifted it into the air and dropped some 1,000 coins on a nearby village.

DID YOU KNOW?

There have been many reports of showers of fish and frogs. On 16 June 1939 a shower of tiny frogs fell at Trowbridge in England. Strong winds had sucked the frogs up from ponds and streams nearby and they then fell with the rain.

Wild weather

Drought
Ice
Wet
Heatwave

In 1972 many places had unusual weather. On the Arctic coast the temperature reached 32°C (90°F) for several days. In the USSR a heatwave caused disastrous forest fires and in India the monsoon rains failed. In Peru and the Philippines, however, there was very heavy rain and flooding.

Television weather maps

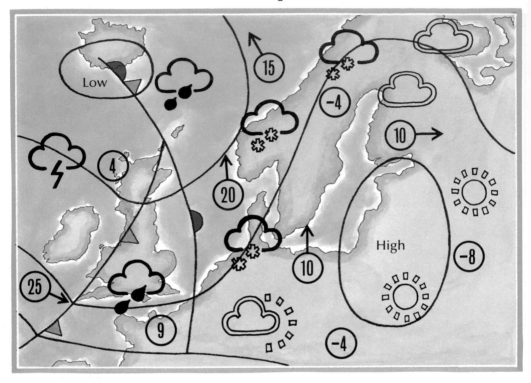

Fronts

warm	
cold	
occluded	

Some weather symbols

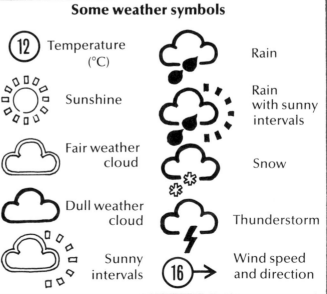

(12)	Temperature (°C)		Rain
	Sunshine		Rain with sunny intervals
	Fair weather cloud		Snow
	Dull weather cloud		Thunderstorm
	Sunny intervals	(16) →	Wind speed and direction

Weather calendar

1st century BC Hero of Alexander (Ancient Greece) was probably the first to discover that air had weight.

1607 The first Frost Fair was held on the frozen river Thames in London with tents, sideshows and foodstalls.

1611 Johann Kepler (Germany) was the first person to describe the six-sided shape of snowflakes.

1643 Evangelista Torricelli (Italy) invented the first barometer for measuring air pressure.

1654 Grand Duke Ferdinand of Tuscany invented the first sealed thermometer for measuring temperature.

1718 Gabriel Daniel Fahrenheit (Germany) devised the Fahrenheit scale (°F) for measuring temperature.

1722 Reverend Horsley (Britain) invented the first modern rain gauge. The earliest mention of a rain gauge is in Indian writings from 400 BC.

1742 Anders Celsius (Sweden) devised the Celsius or Centigrade scale (°C) for measuring temperature.

1752 Benjamin Franklin (USA) invented the lightning conductor for use on high buildings.

1783 Horace-Bénédict de Saussure (Switzerland) made the first hair hygrometer for measuring humidity.

1802 Luke Howard (Britain) named the three families of clouds – cirrus, cumulus and stratus.

1805 Admiral Sir Francis Beaufort (Britain) devised the Beaufort Scale for measuring wind speed at sea.

1843 Lucien Vidie (France) made the first aneroid ('non-liquid') barometer for measuring air pressure.

1846 John Robinson (Britain) invented the cup anemometer for measuring wind speed and direction.

1851 The first published weather maps were sold to the public at the Great Exhibition in London.

1856 The first national storm warning system was started in France after storms destroyed ships during the Crimean War.

c.1887 Clement Wragge (Australia) was the first person to give hurricanes names. They are still named today.

1930 Pierre Molchanov (USSR) launched a radiosonde for measuring weather in the upper atmosphere.

c.1945 John von Neumann (USA) built an electronic computer known as *Maniac.* It was the first to be used for weather forecasting.

1960 The first weather satellite, *Tiros I,* was launched by the USA.

Weather record breakers

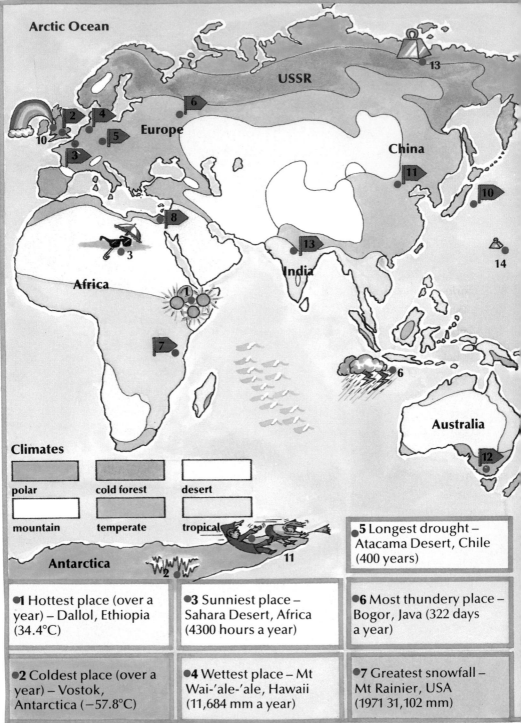

Arctic Ocean

USSR

Europe

China

13

6

11

10

Africa

8

3

India

13

14

1

7

6

Australia

12

Climates

polar   cold forest   desert

mountain   temperate   tropical

Antarctica   11

2

5 Longest drought –
Atacama Desert, Chile
(400 years)

●**1** Hottest place (over a
year) – Dallol, Ethiopia
(34.4°C)

●**3** Sunniest place –
Sahara Desert, Africa
(4300 hours a year)

●**6** Most thundery place –
Bogor, Java (322 days
a year)

●**2** Coldest place (over a
year) – Vostok,
Antarctica (–57.8°C)

●**4** Wettest place – Mt
Wai-'ale-'ale, Hawaii
(11,684 mm a year)

●**7** Greatest snowfall –
Mt Rainier, USA
(1971 31,102 mm)

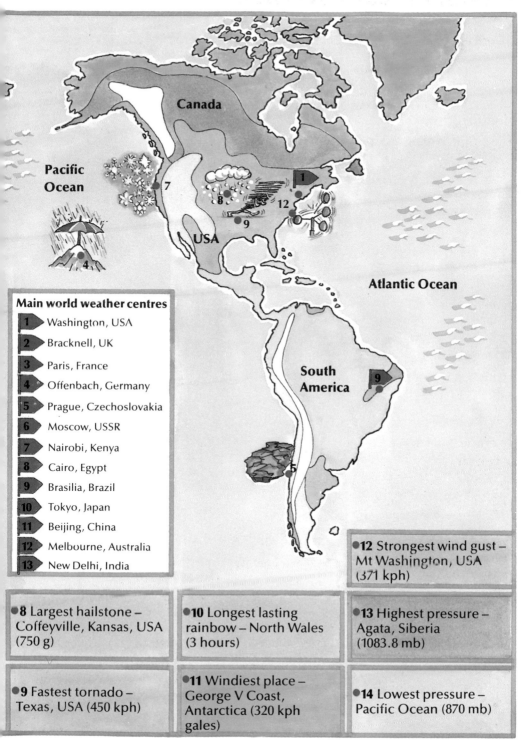

Canada

Pacific
Ocean

7

USA

8

12

9

1

Atlantic Ocean

South
America

9

5

Main world weather centres

1 Washington, USA
2 Bracknell, UK
3 Paris, France
4 Offenbach, Germany
5 Prague, Czechoslovakia
6 Moscow, USSR
7 Nairobi, Kenya
8 Cairo, Egypt
9 Brasilia, Brazil
10 Tokyo, Japan
11 Beijing, China
12 Melbourne, Australia
13 New Delhi, India

12 Strongest wind gust –
Mt Washington, USA
(371 kph)

8 Largest hailstone –
Coffeyville, Kansas, USA
(750 g)

10 Longest lasting
rainbow – North Wales
(3 hours)

13 Highest pressure –
Agata, Siberia
(1083.8 mb)

9 Fastest tornado –
Texas, USA (450 kph)

11 Windiest place –
George V Coast,
Antarctica (320 kph
gales)

14 Lowest pressure –
Pacific Ocean (870 mb)

Glossary

Air mass Huge mass of cold or warm air which moves around the world. Can be dry or moist.

Air pressure The weight of the atmosphere pressing down on the Earth's surface.

Anemometer Instrument used to measure wind speed.

Atmosphere The blanket of air around the Earth.

Barometer Instrument used to measure air pressure.

Celsius Degrees (°C) used for measuring temperature. Also called Centigrade.

Climate The general weather of a place over a long period of time.

Cloud A mass of tiny water droplets or ice crystals.

Cold front Boundary between two different air masses where cold air pushes warm air away. Usually means colder weather.

Condensation When water vapour cools and turns into liquid water.

Coriolis effect The bending of the winds caused by the Earth spinning on its axis.

Dew point The temperature at which the air cannot hold any more water vapour and condensation begins.

Evaporation When liquid water is heated and turns into water vapour.

Fahrenheit Degrees (°F) used for measuring temperature.

High (anticyclone) Area of high pressure. Brings dry weather.

Humidity The amount of moisture in the form of water vapour there is in the air.

Hygrometer Instrument used to measure humidity.

Isobars Lines drawn on a weather map, joining places of equal pressure.

Jet stream Strong wind 5-10 km up in the atmosphere.

Low (depression) Area of low pressure. Often brings wet weather.

Meteorology The scientific study of the atmosphere and weather.

Meteorologists Scientists who study the atmosphere and weather.

Millibar Unit (mb) used to measure air pressure.

Occluded front Combination of warm and cold fronts as cold air overtakes warm front.

Precipitation Water which falls from a cloud as rain, snow or hail.

Radiosonde Instruments attached to a balloon for measuring the weather in the upper atmosphere.

Synoptic chart Weather map using isobars to show highs, lows and fronts.

Thermometer Instrument used to measure temperature.

Troposphere The lowest level of the atmosphere, directly above the ground, where weather happens.

Warm front Boundary between two different air masses where warm air pushes cold air away to bring warmer weather.

Water vapour Water in gas form which is in the atmosphere and helps make the weather.

Weather The state of the air at a certain time and place. Temperature, humidity, wind, cloud and precipitation.

Index